Carrytale Cottage

by

Richard MacNeill

for
my Sunflower and my Superhero

"Carrytale Cottage"
Copyright by Richard MacNeill
Illustrations by Murton Arts
www.BuaidhArts.com

Once upon a time, there lived a poet with his two children
on the edge of a magic forest.

The Faerydust Purse

The poet with his two children Iz and Os were returning with a basketful of berries when a faery in the lavender appeared and said, *"A gift for your daughter."* She held out a little purse with painted flowers and brass buckle and gave simple instructions, *"She may put within it flowers, herbs, leaves of her choosing and hang it somewhere safe, and its blessings will turn the contents to faerydust. She can spread the magic as she wanders through forests and fields and will always be known as a friend of the fae."*

Iz was so excited with the present, she began immediately gathering herbs and leaves from the garden. When the magic turned it to faerydust, she tossed it everywhere as she danced. In a turn of the moon, however, she began to misuse the gift, teasing her brother Os whenever he asked to see inside.

Her father warned, *"Be kind. Magic does not like to be flaunted and the faeries detest such mortal vanity."* But, she continued taunting and when her brother came near to touch the purse she flailed it at him like an unruly weapon. It struck his little hand and her father spoke again, *"You will hurt those closest to you and yourself when you are not respectful with your gifts."* Still, she did not heed his advice. Her brother came near and she swung it again. The cord snapped like a whip unexpectedly and the purse hit her head, *whump,* then she and the purse were gone!

Her father and brother searched for her through the house and garden. Nearing sunset, they heard the faintest voice calling from the climbing jasmine vines. It was Iz in the form of a tiny yellow spider with clear eyes. Her father and brother stayed beside her as she wove a web in the green, bushy leaves and fragrant starflowers.

Alas! Happy this is not the end of the tale. It is told how the yellow spider-lass went from her abode to help Neverbug the Wanderer travel over the bright web of stars and returned restored with the faerydust purse slung over her shoulder. Walking into the cottage, she called to her father and brother who embraced her with smiles and hugs and kisses.

※

Oh, here's my glass of water.
Ice all melted already?
Slurp
Hm, tastes funny,
almost like watermelon.
No, grapes.
Slurp
Aha! It's distinctly the taste
of grubby toddler fingers.

※

Hearts and rainbows
adorn our home
in perfect symmetry.
Where the sage hangs,
I watch the dragon's laughter
and afternoon rain
as we take off our shoes and socks
and feel alive again.

※

The peach tree growing
with my children,
the humble laughter
and smiles.
Summer heat,
water their game,
playing and singing,
splashing and squawking.
Nothing more wholesome
on this planet
than my children
on their heads in the mud.

Little Faery

Little faery sittin' on my windowsill
with the eyes of a searcher
Little faery sittin' on my windowsill
she can't sit still
'cause she's got the wings to fly and fly she will
Oh, yes she will

Little faery sittin' on my windowsill
with the heart of a healer
Little faery sittin' on my windowsill
she won't sit still
'cause there is a life to live and she will live
Yes, she will live

And she'll always be that little faery on my windowsill

Daughters

-are every man's
dream come true,
the prettiest girl
in the world
and always happy
to see you.

Wax-butt

These are **MY** crayons!
I'll sit on them
so no one can take them away.

Don't you know, little girl,
you can't enjoy crayons that way?

Rhys to the Rescue!

I have a sword
(okay, it's a stick)
With this I protect our house
from goblins and from getting sick
My sister, she is a magic one
with healing in her hands
and I am the bravest warrior
in all these changing lands
I was born a superhero
It is my destiny
Rhys to the Rescue!
is what I shout
loud as the roaring sea
Daddy teaches me the way
to use this weapon properly
Not for debate or cutting trees
there's only one reason we carry swords-
protecting the family

A Dragon In My Backpack

There's a dragon in my backpack
I brought it to school with me
It likes to hide in my brother's room
And comes out when we're having tea
He's a cute little pal, fits in my hand
I call him Grundie and this is my plan
When we all go out to recess
I'll unzip my bag and set him free
Then all the kids in my class
Will want to play with me
But, Grundie is protective
He knows who's false and who is true
So don't pretend to be my friend
Or he'll come after you
At lunch I'll hide him in my pocket
And slip him slurps of applesauce
Then out in the breeze
Growing on trees
Are pinecones we can toss
His teeth are sharp, his hide is rough
His eyes bulge out like this
His wings are tough
And that's enough
To be a friend to any who wish

The Hard Return Home

Early morning was spent fighting off goblins who tried to raid the kitchen. Later when they were out in the garden, the poet transformed into a tall white horse. His children hopped up on his back and they rode once around the giant beanstalk, then galloped into the magic forest. As they were playing in the leaves and jumping on rocks, their father looked up into a bare tree and saw something awaiting the right druid-eyes. He climbed to the highest branches and the children learned, while he unwrapped the magic staff from its dry bark, of their mystic abode in the home of seasons and the great song which keeps them alive. Then, they gathered kindling for the hearth and made their way home.

Striding over the grassy hills near a blue lake, they suddenly heard a loud rumble and turned to see an angry giant fuming toward them. *"In the water!"* Os shouted, running to the lake and throwing his armload of kindling at the bank. The poet watched, smiling. He knew this giant. Iz swung a big stick, distracting it in circles until her brother emerged splashing with two extra arms! He had a riverbow with arrows and their father's battle-beaten shield. Above his head, he shook a rattle into a spell of sgian dubh. *"No, giant!"* he bravely yelled as it lumbered to squish his sister. Together, they beat and chased the behemoth stomping over the hill. *"Daddy, did you see what we did?!"* they hooted, and the poet was happy to see their bravery.

Nearing the edge of the forest, they passed a band of goblins hoping to sneak into the kitchen once more. Father and children fell hard on the heads of those dark-deed-doers and sent them screeching away. Then, gathering up their scattered bundles of kindling, they were home before twilight.

Thought there was a werewolf

Walking to the linen closet
to fetch myself a towel,
my daughter in her bed
in the shadows of her room
suddenly began to wail.
I looked in the doorway
as she howled, "Werewolf!"
she cried, "Werewolf!"
I stepped in with words of concern
closer to where she lay.
Seeing me, she crawled up the wall
yelling like a frightened bean-sidhe
and I realized to my dismay
the werewolf she saw
was me.

Ant Pizza

I set the box down
to kindle a fire;
camping, but with a
pre-purchased meal.
Then, I opened the lid
and found some additions.
Would they be peppery?
Would they be sweet?
To the feast we partook.
Both to be eating.
Both to be eaten
as I had the first taste
of ant pizza

Oatmeal

Oatmeal's sticking everywhere,
even to my mouth.
Oatmeal's what I like to wear
when travelling east, north, west, and south.
I wear oatmeal when I'm going to school,
a bit on my lapel adds color.
Is there some in my hair?
Oatmeal's sticking everywhere.

Jumping Robot

I'm a jumping robot!
I bounce from the bed
to the floor
to the walls
till the whole world around
keeps going up and down
even when I've stopped.
My springs are new,
my lights and gears too.
But my equilibrium
is a tad askew.
Oops, now I'm a falling robot.

Oh Little Boy

Oh little boy you cannot walk yet
but you move just fine
and I can see it in your handsome face
that you're gonna shine
Oh little boy you cannot talk yet
no you don't say a thing
but I can hear it in your cute little laugh
that you're gonna sing
Oh little boy
you've got to grow up big and strong for your daddy
but don't forget to stay little for your mommy

Ziggity bop bop diddily doe, deedee deet dot diddily dye
Ziggity bop bop diddily dop bop ba deedee dada deet da diddily dye

Oh yes, my little boy, I will teach you all I know
and I will take you out into the world and
I will show you the love and the light
and the joys and the fights and
you will be a better man than I could ever hope to be
My heart for you is an ocean
so sail away on adventure
'cause you know that I'll be with you everyday
in your spirit, in your freedom
in the sun and in the sky
in the earth under your feet
and in the stars at night

Ziggity bop bop diddily doe, deedee deet dot diddily dye
Ziggity bop bop diddily dop bop ba deedee dada deet da diddily dye

Doodoo doo doo

A Day Which Freedom Bears

Smoke from their chimney rose and travelled through the forest trees. Iz was gathering berries and firewood while her father and brother were training in swordplay. As the poet was showing a few detailed points of close combat, a horde of wily pandas came jumping out of the tall trees hungry for the freshly picked berries. Os stood before them and howled, *"Do not cross these blades, you bears!"* The pandas, surprised, bounced off.

They continued their play until the pandas returned, walking slowly and solemnly through the mist of the trees. The one who led them carried a long blade of amethyst laid out in his hands. *"Young man,"* he said, *"we thank you for your bravery and give you this gift."* Os looked at his father, who nodded. He stepped forward and accepted the sword, thanking them and lifting high the shining purple blade.

That afternoon, they went over the fields to an enchanted tea garden. Quiet, serene, simple among tables and trellises, they were served by a kind and patient monk who advised peppermint tea and scones topped with cinnamon butter. The poet drank his tea smiling while his son enjoyed butter by the knife-load and his daughter gulped down three sugary cups before retiring to dress formally in the Princess Room. Her brother was admitted into the lounge upon his willingness to play dress-up.

With hugs, they departed the monk's company and made their way home to complete the fun day. They entered the bouncy palace within their cottage where music plays from the air. A silver elephant from Iz's room joined them and from Os's room came two bow-tie bears. They jumped and danced and sang, silly and happy as rolly-pollies in a patch of clover.

The Cat Children

After a bright sunset,
as the sky was darkening,
the poet emerged with new poems
tied into scrolls which he hung
in trees for anyone to find and read.
Four children with an old wagon
came rolling out of the forest.
They looked hungry
and not quite lost, but knowing they were
out of place.
They played and talked with each other
and when they noticed the poet
they asked where they could find fresh water.
He told them where the stream runs pure
and they remained at the edge of the trees another moment
talking and playing in the gathering twilight.
Having some extra bread,
he brought them a basket full.
But when he returned from inside the cottage,
four cats were skulking around
much like the children he had seen.
He wrapped the loaves and placed them
in the old wagon.
Later in the evening when he went out
to look at the stars,
the wagon was gone
and he could see footprints
of the cat children
where they'd changed shape and moved on.

Rain rain
wash away

Slow us down
to see our day

Whether you say...

    Grandfather wolf laughed, his long grey fur swaying in the breeze as cubs and parents wrestled beside the entrance of their cave. Mother and Sister wolf returned from deep in the forest and told them where they'd found a meadow of flowers and butterflies. Daddy wolf told Grandmother quietly about the herd of antelope he'd scouted during the night.

    As he silently stalked away, Grandmother guided the cubs behind him. Over a gorge he leaped and caught an antelope on the far side. The cubs watched as he guarded the meal and they asked, *"How are we going to get over there? We can't jump that far."*

    Grandmother wolf smiled, *"Whether you say you can or you can't, you're right."* The feistiest young one confidently lifted an eyebrow and ran toward the gorge. Grandmother wolf caught him by the tail and pointed to where a wide, fallen tree made a bridge to the other side.

The Eternal Forest

In the wild the child lives,
of startling appearance
with bright face, mischievous hair,
and piercing, smiling eyes.
Shockingly swift, running and jumping
and climbing high, keeping pace with the animals,
laughing and free, the child dances in grassy clearings
while birds flutter and tweet.
At midday the child might be found swimming and splashing
in a pond 'neath the stream
or resting on a forest bed of lichen and leaves.
Singing with pixies, talking with gnomes,
petting the unicorn, thus
is the destiny of the child.
Climbing through the trees,
the child came across a crowd of humans,
big and loud and terrifying.
Shouting. Noise. Noise. Shouting
as they cut and burned the woods,
paving hard, black roads.
Many roads had begun
to slither through the forest,
all with signs, all black and barren.
The yellers are frightened of the wild
where the child frolics joyfully
and sleeps in peaceful comfort.
They do not see the beauty of the world
as they search for life and truth.
Some reach where the end of their path
empties into the trees, and as they
are found they remain lost
and make more roads or go to find
what they missed along the way.
The wild from where the path begins
is the wild where the path ends

and they are distracted
with quick-moving glances
and seek not within.
Sometimes, the child sits up in the trees
watching those who do not stop moving,
and sincerely wishes the best for them.
The finding is the flowing clear water,
the wild child leaping into the pond
and rising as everlasting
in the Eternal Forest.

Tir Solas

In the night, goblins were attracted from their lairs by the boy's screaming. He didn't want to go to bed. They broke through the wall into the cottage, but the poet was ready and beat them back, punching and kicking and grappling them through the hole, then sealed it up with a slab of furniture which broke in the fray. He heard them scurry down far below, then cast an orb of shining blue light from himself all around, expanding to surround their entire home until it shielded the garden, the land underneath, and the sky above. The carrytale cottage was protected by this father's magic, and he went to tell his children they were safe. *"But, you must stop screaming,"* he said to his son, *"or you will continue to call them forth."*

The next morning, while Iz and Os were climbing trees, an old man from another realm who'd steadily been roaming closer to the forest, turned on his machine. It thundered and smoked and stank of an evil they'd never seen. With it, he cut down a tree and left it in the grass. The children could hear the tree crying, and when the man saw them high in the branches, he yelled at them to get down. They ignored him until he went away grumbling, and when he was gone over the hill, they went to hug the stump. They could still smell the dark smoke mixing with the clean, blue air and they rushed home to tell their father what happened.

The next day, the man came and sawed up the trunk, then gathered a wheelbarrow full before the wood was even dry. He cut the roots where they were tucked into the ground, then hitched a bigger machine to it and pulled and pulled it out. If you are one who can hear the trees speak, you would have heard a pain you could never imagine.

He saw the two children in the trees and again yelled at them to get down. This time Os shouted back, *"No!"* and the man walked away with a growl. When he was gone, the children jumped down and ran home to their father. In the evening, they gathered the stump and what remained of the wood before it could be taken, the machine still sitting there in the dark.

The poet and his children stayed home the next day, wary of going where the man was invading. On the next, they went to the far quiet canyon to make a new besom. They brought a tall staff and gathered sweetgrass and tied it with flowers of autumn. From upon the biggest boulder, they tossed offerings of thanks to the great song. Then they hopped on the broom, held tight, and flew home.

When the children and their father returned to the edge of the magic forest, they saw three trees had been ripped from the ground and a little white fence had been built between the woods and the field. The poet began gathering seeds while his children climbed above him. After a while, they heard a man shout, "You need to get down from that tree."

The poet turned and yelled to the man, *"These are my children and they can climb trees!"* The old man replied that he too climbed trees when he was a young child, but didn't want them to fall "on his property" for fear that some damages may occur to the home he had yet to build. The poet was sickened by the uncaring cruelty of the meant-to-be-elder who denied what he knew was right and good and replaced it with the hate and fear of self-serving ways, who did not care for life at all, only for his possessions. Toward the old man, the poet raised his hands and protected his children with a mighty spell-

"This Is Not Your Forest and
You Will Not Stay and brand
Every Tree You See On Land
for Our Ways are the Oldest and
You Are Trespassing... Sand
Will Rise and Sink You In
until You are No More; you're bland!"

As he shouted, the man began to shrink and walked away over the fields. The children continued climbing while their father gathered the seeds of trees. Eventually, Os did fall and hurt his knee, and as his father comforted him, he laughed and rolled his eyes at the irony. But, the man could no longer curse this land. They picked the boy up and dusted him off, wiped his tears, and in a moment he was laughing again. The poet with his daughter and son each planted a seed in the soil where the trees were ripped out, then returned home.

As the children slept in the night, their father went out in the moonlight to cast a spell strong enough to make their cottage castle-tight. Around the magic forest- Tír Solas, Land of Light -he made their home safe away from all mortal plight. His vision reached to the sea where he saw a goddess on the beach whom he would meet and his children greet with love and great adventure, all the way into mountains green where joy would root and sail and gleam, he saw it, a protected dream.

In the morning, they stepped out and the dawn was pink under bright waves of sunrise. They walked carefully and peered through the trees. Then, the poet and his children smiled and cheered when they saw the white fence had disappeared and from the ripped-out holes in the ground were growing three saplings, strong, happy, and proud.

And they lived happily ever after

www.ingramcontent.com/pod-product-compliance
Lightning Source LLC
Chambersburg PA
CBHW042002050726
47507CB00030B/201